# DISNEY'S ENCHANTING STORIES

## DISNEY'S HERCULES in A TORCH FOR MEG

INSIDE

PG-4

S0-ARA-743

WRITTEN BY **D. G. CHICHESTER**

PENCILED BY **TOD SMITH**

INKED BY **STEVE GEORGE**

**JANICE CHIANG**
Letterer

**HEROIC AGE STUDIOS**
Colorists

**VALERIE D'ORAZIO**
Assistant Editor

**EVAN SKOLNICK**
AYR Group Editor

**FABIAN NICIEZA**
Editor-in-Chief

**Beauty and the Beast in THE ART CRITIC**

**PG·46**

Written by **Bob Budiansky**

Penciled by **Bill Neville**

Inked by **Phyllis Novin**

**The Hunchback of Notre Dame in ON THE HORNS OF A DILEMMA**

**PG·54**

Written by **Michael Gallagher**

Penciled by **Mike Kazaleh**

Inked by **Steve George**

President/Publisher **Fabian Nicieza** • Director of Business Affairs **Hayley Eden** • AYR Marketing Director/Product Manager **Stacy Lowe** • Circulation Manager **Lee Hansen** Marketing Coordinator **Stephen Vrattos** • Production Manager/Design Director **Scott Friedlander** • Operations Manager **James Perham** • Senior Graphic Designer **Joe Caponsacco** • Graphic Designers **Ray Leung, Jade Moede** • AYR Intern **Harvey Richards III**

275 Seventh Ave 14th Fl
New York, NY 10001
212 366 4900

**acclaim**
**BOOKS**

**ayr**
**acclaim**
**young readers**

I'M *SORRY* FOR WHAT YOU'VE GONE THROUGH, TYPHOS, I REALLY *AM...*

...BUT I *CAN'T* JUST *LOOK* THE OTHER WAY WHEN YOU *STEAL* OUR TORCH!

I UNDERSTAND... I *DON'T* WANT MY *FAMILY* THINKING THAT THEIR OLD LIZARD IS A *THIEF!*

# "ZERO TO HERO"
## DECODER SWEEPSTAKES

A=🏹  B=🏹
C=⚱  D=🗡  E=⚫  F=🔥
G=🍇  H=⛑  I=🏺  J=👑  K=🔷  L=🎵
M=🪞  N=🐚  O=🥚  P=🌿  Q=❓  R=☁
S=◎  T=🏆  U=🐭  V=🌿  W=〜  X=▤
Y=🚣  Z=⚡

Enter Disney's "Zero to Hero" Sweepstakes for a chance to win one of these great prizes:

**GRAND PRIZE: A trip for a family of four to Greece!**

**1ST PRIZE**
10 Winners - *Hercules* Sericel from Walt Disney Art Classics

**2ND PRIZE**
25 Winners - Assorted Disney's *Hercules* Toys by Mattel

**3RD PRIZE**
100 Winners - Disney's *Hercules* Soundtrack from Walt Disney Records.

# WHO GOES FROM ZERO TO HERO?

⬜ ⬜ ⬜ ⬜ ⬜ ⬜ ⬜ ⬜

**Name** (18 years and older)_____ **Date of Birth**___/___/___

**Address**_____ **City**_____

**State**_____ **Zip**_____ **Daytime Phone Number** (____)_____

**No purchase necessary. Prizes - Trip to Greece for 4 (approx. retail value: $7,000.00), 10 Winners - *Hercules* Sericel from Disney Art Classics, 25 Winners - Assorted Disney's *Hercules* Toys by Mattel, 100 Winners - Disney's *Hercules* Soundtrack from Walt Disney Records.**

WHAT CAN A RACCOON DO TO LEND A PAW?

FLIT AND PERCY ARE ENLISTED FOR A QUEST THROUGH THE NEIGHBORING WOODS.

CHITTER CHITTER!

29

AND THE DRESS?

IT'S, IT'S...

TERRIBLE, I KNOW. AND A WASTE OF GOOD BUCKSKIN! WE MAY AS WELL CUT IT UP FOR *RAGS!*

ALL OUR EFFORTS ARE *NOTHING* WITHOUT SKILL--

FATHER! ER, WHAT A *SURPRISE* TO SEE YOU!

SO I HAD *INTENDED!*

⸓ tsk ⸓ THAT DRESS HAS SEEN ITS DAY. YOU SHOULD RETIRE IT.

IT WILL MAKE GOOD *RAGS,* THOUGH.

OH. YES, FATHER! AS YOU SAY...

I HAVE *BROUGHT* YOU SOMETHING, CHILD. AND I'VE WAITED MANY YEARS FOR THIS MOMENT!

FOR *ME?*

OH, FATHER! MY *MOTHER'S DRESS!*

YOU ARE *PLEASED?*

PLEASED... AND *RELIEVED!*

I WILL WEAR IT WITH SUCH *PRIDE* IN THE PAGEANT--

OH! *MORE* VISITORS!

JUST WHAT HAVE *YOU THREE* BEEN UP TO?

A LILY.... A THISTLE... ACORNS...

*I* UNDERSTAND. YOU HEARD ME DESCRIBE THE DRESS!

THESE ARE LOVELY THINGS, AND I'D WEAR THEM *MYSELF,* BUT--

33

# SAVE $10.00 ON

# ENCHANTMENT!

**SAVE $10.00 OFF THE RETAIL PRICE WHEN YOU SUBSCRIBE TO DISNEY'S ENCHANTING STORIES! THAT'S LIKE GETTING TWO ISSUES FREE!**

EACH ENCHANTING STORYBOOK FEATURES 64 FULL-COLOR PAGES OF YOUR FAVORITE DISNEY CHARACTERS IN ALL-NEW FUN-FILLED ADVENTURES! ENJOY HOURS OF READING FUN WITH YOUR FRIENDS FROM BEAUTY AND THE BEAST, POCAHONTAS, SNOW WHITE AND THE SEVEN DWARFS, HERCULES, 101 DALMATIANS, AND THE HUNCHBACK OF NOTRE DAME!

---

## YES! PLEASE SEND ME 6 ISSUES OF
### DISNEY'S ENCHANTING STORIES FOR ONLY $17.00.
I UNDERSTAND THAT I'LL SAVE A TOTAL OF $10.00 OFF THE COVER PRICE!

(PLEASE PRINT)

NAME _____

ADDRESS _____

CITY _____

STATE _____ ZIP _____

SEND A CHECK OR MONEY ORDER PAYABLE TO
**ACCLAIM BOOKS**
(NY RESIDENTS, PLEASE ADD APPLICABLE SALES TAX.)
PHOTOCOPIES OF THIS FORM ARE ACCEPTABLE.
SORRY - NOT AVAILABLE TO RESIDENTS OF CANADA.

SEND TO:
ACCLAIM BOOKS
YOUNG READER
SUBSCRIPTIONS
PO BOX 40
VERNON, NJ 07462

**OFFER EXPIRES 11/30/97**

© Disney

KEY CODE 02K

THE END

MADEMOISELLE, YOU MUST *DO SOMETHING!*

THE MASTER WILL BE VERY *UPSET* IF ANY OF HIS ARTWORK IS DAMAGED!

I SUPPOSE YOU'RE *RIGHT.* THE BEAST DOES HAVE A *TEMPER.*

THAT'S ENOUGH! WE'RE *LEAVING...*AND WE'RE *LOCKING THE DOOR* SO NO ONE CAN EVER COME IN HERE AGAIN TO *ADMIRE* ALL OF YOU!

YOU WOULDN'T--!

WITHOUT ADMIRERS, WE... WE'D FEEL SO *WORTHLESS!*

YES. I SUPPOSE YOU WOULD.

BUT PERHAPS IF YOU ALL LEARNED TO *GET ALONG* BETTER...

...WE WOULD COME BACK.

I'LL TRY IF *YOU* WILL.

VERY WELL...

AND YOU DON'T NEED TO LOOK SO ANGRY.

PEOPLE WILL *STILL* RESPECT YOU, EVEN IF YOU SMILE.

YOU...YOU REALLY *THINK* SO?

AND I DIDN'T MEAN TO UPSET YOU BEFORE. I JUST THOUGHT A HAPPIER FACE WOULD MAKE YOU LOOK EVEN MORE BEAUTIFUL.

THAT'S... THAT'S A GOOD IDEA. THANK YOU.

THE HUNCHBACK OF NOTRE DAME

LOOK! THERE GOES ESMERALDA IN HER GYPSY WAGON... I RECOGNIZE IT!

**THE END**

# FREE ISSUE JUST FOR KIDS!

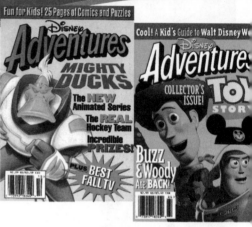

Fun for Kids! 25 Pages of Comics and Puzzles

Disney Adventures MIGHTY DUCKS — The NEW Animated Series — The REAL Hockey Team — Incredible PRIZES! — PLUS BEST FALL TV

Cool! A Kid's Guide to Walt Disney World — Disney Adventures — COLLECTOR'S ISSUE! — TOY STORY — Buzz & Woody Are BACK!

## Disney Adventures

is the super-charged, super-fun magazine that a whopping one million kids ages 7-14 love to read each month! That's because, DA is jam-packed with super-cool stuff they care about. **Things like...**

The inside scoop on Big-Time **MOVIE STARS** & awesome **ATHLETES** ✪ Hot, new **VIDEO GAMES**...and how to beat 'em ✪ Fun **IDEAS** for things to do indoors and out ✪ Must-see **MOVIES** ✪ Great new **MUSIC** ✪ The **CHARACTERS** they love ✪ Brain-bending **PUZZLES** ✪ Crazy **CONTESTS** ✪ Wacky **FACTS** to impress friends ✪ Inspiring **STORIES ABOUT KIDS** like them ✪ Kooky **COMICS** and much, much more!

## SEND FOR YOUR FREE ISSUE TODAY!